SpongeBob had invited his Bikini Bottom pals over to his house for a surprise. Mr. Krabs thought it would be a free-money party, Sandy thought it was going to be a science fair, and Larry the Lobster expected a weight lifting competition.

"I'm really glad you could all make it," said SpongeBob happily. "Tonight is going to be a magical evening filled with . . . an entire reel of my family vacation!"

Everyone immediately headed for the door . . . until SpongeBob showed the first slide.

SPONGEBOB'S RUNAWAY ROAD TRIP SLIDES

SpongeBob's vacation with his parents and Patrick started off like any other family road trip. They were headed to the Great Barrier Reef, where there were all sorts of slides, trampolines, and ropes to swing on. It was going to be the best vacation ever!

"Let's all sing the 'Road Song,'" suggested Mrs. SquarePants.

"Great idea! *When I'm on the road I see stuff going by . . . ,*" SpongeBob sang happily.

"*Road! Road! Road!*" chanted Patrick.

Things were going really great—until their boat suddenly broke down and they had to take it to a service station. While waiting for the boat to be fixed, SpongeBob and Patrick played in an old playground nearby. It wasn't the Great Barrier Reef, but they tried to make the best of it.

"Hey, look! Swings!" exclaimed SpongeBob. "Try it, Patrick!"

Patrick got on and swung so high that it broke away from the swing set. He fell and started to slide down a giant drainpipe.

"I'm coming to help, buddy!" yelled SpongeBob as he jumped into the drain.

"Woohoo! That was awesome!" yelled Patrick when he landed at the bottom of the drain. "Let's do it again!"

"Um, Patrick, I think that was a one-way drain," said SpongeBob.

SpongeBob and Patrick wandered around, not sure where they were. The place was filled with all sorts of strange plants and sounds. They were definitely off the beaten path!

Moments later they heard a loud grumbling sound. Something was hungry and it wasn't Patrick or SpongeBob! It had to be a huge monster!

SpongeBob and Patrick ran as fast as they could and soon came to a cliff with a steep drop. They had to choose between jumping or being eaten alive—so they jumped!

After what seemed like a very long fall, they landed on something bouncy and springy.

"Patrick, we did it!" said SpongeBob as they bounced along.

"We're not going to be eaten!" cheered Patrick.

"Put 'er there, pal," said SpongeBob as he did a happy little dance with his eyes closed. But when SpongeBob opened his eyes, he couldn't believe what he saw. Standing behind Patrick was a gigantic fruit fly!

"What? Is it time to scream again?" Patrick asked a stunned SpongeBob.

Quickly, SpongeBob and Patrick swung on some vines to get away from the fruit fly.

They got away just in time!

"Patrick, this vacation is a disaster!" cried SpongeBob.

Patrick thought for a moment. "I don't think it's a disaster," he said happily. "We did everything we dreamed of doing at the Great Barrier Reef. We went down a huge drain pipe like a slide, bounced around like on trampolines, then swung on some vines which are kinda like ropes!"

"You're right!" exclaimed SpongeBob. "This vacation had it all!"

MR. KRABS TAKES A VACATION

Who's ready for some excitement? Then hold on to your coin purses, here are my vacation slides!

Mr. Krabs's vacation started when he invited SpongeBob to join him and Pearl on a tour of the Bikini Bottom Mint, where all the money in Bikini Bottom is made.

"Have you ever seen anything more beautiful in all your life?" asked Mr. Krabs when they arrived.

"Daddy, this is not a vacation!" said Pearl angrily. "I wanted to go to Mega Mall World or the Teenage Boy Museum. I'm not going in there!" And she stomped off.

"Guess it's just you and me, laddie," Mr. Krabs told SpongeBob. "Me, you . . . and all that money!"

"Hello. I will be your guide today," said Bill, the tour guide. "This is the first part of the dollar-making process, where very special sheets of paper are prepped for printing. . . ."

"And this area is where sheets of silver are turned into batches of shiny coins. . . ."

Mr. Krabs shook with excitement.

"Get a hold of yourself Mr. Krabs," said SpongeBob. "It's just sheets of paper and silver!"

"*Just* paper and silver? That's like saying the ocean is *just* water, or a Krabby Patty is *just* a sandwich," said Mr. Krabs as his head started to spin.

"Ahem. Can we continue?" Bill asked impatiently as he waited for Mr. Krabs to calm down. "Now, over here is the machine where we destroy old money by shredding it—"

"Noooo!" yelled Mr. Krabs as he started to cry. "Why would anyone destroy money?!"

"It's okay, sir," said SpongeBob. "The shredded money is recycled and turned into brand-new money!"

"That's it!" yelled Bill. "I've had enough of you two interrupting the tour."

And that's when everyone noticed the two masked robbers!

"Oh, no ya don't! No one steals a dollar in front of me!" yelled Mr. Krabs. He lunged toward the masked robbers and, with SpongeBob's help, managed to tie them up and fling them out the window and onto an oncoming police car. It was the easiest arrest in Bikini Bottom history.

"You are both brave citizens," said Bill, "and for that, on behalf of the Mint, I would like to present you each with brand-new limited-edition dollar bills with your faces on them."

"Ooooh . . . ," SpongeBob and Mr. Krabs said. Just then Pearl appeared and snatched the bills.

"I'll take those," she said as she handed them to a sales clerk. "I was short two dollars for these adorable boots. Don't you love them, Daddy?"

SANDY'S MOONCATION

"Okay, this here first slide is of me gettin' some last-minute readings before I took off for my vacation to the moon," said Sandy as she started her vacation slides.

For her exciting trip to the moon Sandy had carefully planned out everything—everything, that is, except for SpongeBob accidently stowing away on the rocket ship.

"SpongeBob! What in cold chicken 'n' pickles are you doing on my rocket ship?" asked Sandy when she saw SpongeBob.

"I came to bring you a going-away cake!" said SpongeBob, pleased with himself.

"Oh, goodness. Well, countdown's already started. . . . ," said Sandy exasperated. "Strap yourself in; you're going on a mooncation."

The first thing on Sandy's vacation agenda: moon crater boarding. Sandy showed SpongeBob all her best moves, from the Texas Tail Grab to the Tour de Saturn. Then it was SpongeBob's turn, but instead of moving down the moon crater, SpongeBob started floating up—the zero gravity was really affecting him!

Sandy lassoed a rock onto SpongeBob to help him out. It worked! By holding on to the rock, SpongeBob was able to do some really great moves.

"Wow, SpongeBob! Whad'ya call that trick?" asked an impressed Sandy.

"Whaaaa!" yelled SpongeBob as he passed by.

Suddenly, SpongeBob lost control of the board and it crashed into the rocket's fuel tank! There was no time to lose. Sandy and SpongeBob had to get back on the rocket ship before it ran out of fuel. As they headed back to Bikini Bottom, the rocket ship started to lose control and Sandy jumped out to steer the ship.

Thankfully, the rocket made it back to Earth.

"Oh, Sandy. I'm so sorry I ruined your vacation to the moon," said SpongeBob sadly.

"Ruined? No way! That was the most fun I've had in a toad's age!" Sandy exclaimed. "Next time we're vacationing on Mars!"

WALKING THE PLANKTON

Salutations, puny mortals! You will endure my vacation slides!

Plankton's vacation was supposed to be a second honeymoon with his wife, Karen . . . at least that's what Karen thought. The truth was that it was another plot by Plankton to steal the Krabby Patty recipe from Mr. Krabs while he was on a week-long cruise.

"Oh, Plankton, this second honeymoon is going to be so great!" exclaimed Karen.

"Yeah, it's going to be groovy, babe. Now, a quick check of the vacation inventory," said Plankton as he packed their suitcase. "Suntan lotion, sunglass, dreaded laser . . . ready!"

On the luxury cruise, Karen and Plankton were soaking up the sun and relaxing.

"You're such a sweet husband, Plankton, when you're not obsessing over that stupid formula," said Karen.

"This is the life," said Plankton as he stretched out on the chair. "Not a care in the world." Secretly though, Plankton was devising a plan on how to steal the Krabby Patty recipe.

Just then a waiter came by and offered them some kelp cheese. This gave Plankton an idea: As Karen slept, he would sculpt the cheese to look like him and sneak away to find Mr. Krabs.

Unfortunately for Plankton, stealing the recipe from Mr. Krabs was going to be harder than getting away from Karen.

First, Plankton planned to steal it while SpongeBob was wheeling Mr. Krabs around on the deck. . . .

Then he tried as SpongeBob and Mr. Krabs were playing shuffleboard, but Plankton ended up flying off on the puck. . . .

Plankton then tried to take down Mr. Krabs while he was waterskiing, but fell overboard instead.

Finally Plankton's big chance came when Mr. Krabs decided to sell Krabby Patties on deck. Dressed in a disguise, Plankton ordered one Krabby Patty and quickly ran off—right into Karen!

"I knew you were up to something!" yelled Karen angrily. "I can't believe you tried to fool me into thinking that this was a second honeymoon!"

"Karen, honey, let me explain," pleaded Plankton as he tried to get away. "Please don't turn on your dreaded laser . . . I'm sooorry!"

PATRICK'S STAYCATION

Sometimes the best vacations are the ones where you don't have to go anywhere or do anything, which is exactly what Patrick wanted to do. It was going to be the best staycation ever—and SpongeBob was going to help!

To kick things off, SpongeBob transformed Patrick's house to look like a resort.

"Welcome to Star Rock Inn, sir," said SpongeBob disguised as a desk clerk. "Here is the key to your room and please do not hesitate to let us know if there is anything we can do to make your stay more comfortable."

"Um, thanks," said Patrick, a little confused.

Before long, Patrick got the hang of asking for things from the "resort." First, he wanted his room rearranged. Then he asked that a diving board be added to the pool. Finally, he wanted a fancy meal, and SpongeBob was only too happy to deliver.

SpongeBob took out his grill and tried to impress Patrick with his fine culinary skills. But he got so carried away that he forgot about the Krabby Patty on the grill—and it burned!

"Wow, you are smokin'!" said Patrick as he pointed to all the smoke behind SpongeBob.

"Aww, it was nothing," said SpongeBob, embarrassed.

After giving Patrick a massage at the "spa," SpongeBob finally headed home to rest. It had been a tiring day helping Patrick relax. As he lay in bed, SpongeBob suddenly heard snoring.

"Patrick, what are you doing here?" asked SpongeBob.

"Oh, the resort next door was too crowded," replied Patrick. "So I found this place. It's quiet and peaceful. Good night, SpongeBob."

As the last slide flashed on the screen, everyone stood up to leave. It had been a long night—a very long night. But apparently not for SpongeBob. . . .

"Now who wants to see our vacation from our vacation?" he asked eagerly.

GREETINGS FROM BIKINI BOTTOM!